ZOO ANIMALS

An Animal Information Book

PRICE/STERN/SLOAN
Publishers, Inc., Los Angeles
1984

Camels have long legs and long necks.

They have one or two humps on their backs.

Camels can store water in their bodies. This means they can live for several days without more water.

The leopard is a member of the cat family.

It has black spots on its coat.

Although a leopard is not as big as a lion or a tiger, it is much more dangerous.

The rhinoceros has very thick skin.

It has one or two horns on its face.

Although a rhinoceros has a heavy body and short legs, it can run very fast.

It eats only grass and plants.

Llamas are members of the same family as camels.

Llamas are smaller than camels and have no humps on their backs.

They have large pointed ears that stick up straight in the air.

Sea lions are excellent swimmers.

They have flippers instead of legs.

Although they can move around on the beach and on rocks, they usually do not go too far from the water.

Sea lions eat fish and other animals found in the ocean.

Tigers have black stripes on their orange coats.

They live in jungles and forests where their coats seem to blend into the trees and grass.

Tigers have large heads and very sharp teeth.

An elephant has a very long trunk. The end of its trunk is its nose. It uses its trunk to pick up food and to carry the food to its mouth. A mother elephant will use her trunk to pick up her baby.

Monkeys are very intelligent animals.

They have hair on their bodies and on their tails.

Monkeys are good tree climbers.

Some of them live in trees.

Monkeys are found in places where the weather is very warm.

Polar bears live in very cold places.

Their white fur makes it difficult for other animals to see them on the snow and ice.

Polar bears are very good hunters.

They are also good fishermen.

Lions are the largest members of the cat family.

They live together in groups called prides. Usually there is one male, and several females and young cubs in each pride.

When they are not hunting, lions enjoy resting in the grass.

The elk is a member of the deer family.

It has very large horns called antlers on its head. The ones on its forehead are usually very sharp.

It likes to eat grass and plants.

The hippopotamus is a member of the pig family.

It is one of the largest of all animals. A hippopotamus can be 12 feet long, stand four or five feet tall, and weigh four tons.

These beautiful birds are called flamingos.

They have long necks and long, very thin legs.

Flamingos live in shallow water.

To eat, they put their beaks upside down on the bottom of the water.

Although it is called a koala bear, this little animal is related to the kangaroo.

The koala lives in trees in Australia.

It has small eyes, large ears and short legs.

Zebras are members of the horse family.

They have large black stripes on their white bodies.

Zebras eat grass and grain.

They live in very large groups called herds.

Zebras travel long distances during the summer to find food and water.

Animal Information Books

Titles in this Series

Baby Animals
Bears
Birds
Farm Animals
Horses & Ponies
Kittens & Cats

Lions & Tigers
Monkeys & Apes
Puppies & Dogs
Sea Animals
Wild Animals
Zoo Animals

Copyright © 1984 Ottenheimer Publishers, Inc.
Published by Price/Stern/Sloan Publishers, Inc.,
410 North La Cienega Boulevard, Los Angeles, California 90048
All Rights Reserved.
Printed in Brazil.
ISBN: 0-8431-1515-7